DATE DUE			9/01
OCT 08 '01			
DEC 07 '01			
FEB 06 '02			
APR 09 '02			
APR 17 '02			
JUL 03 '02			
AUG 2 '02			
AUG 8 '02			
OCT 21 '02			
FEB 27 '03			
APR 1 '03			
MAY 28 '03			
GAYLORD			PRINTED IN U.S.A.

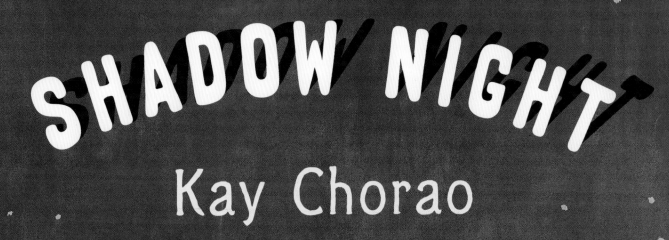

SHADOW NIGHT

Kay Chorao

DUTTON CHILDREN'S BOOKS
New York

Copyright © 2001 by Kay Sproat Chorao
All rights reserved.

CIP Data is available.

Published in the United States 2001 by Dutton Children's Books,
a division of Penguin Putnam Books for Young Readers
345 Hudson Street, New York, New York 10014
www.penguinputnam.com

Designed by Amy Berniker
Printed in Hong Kong
First Edition
1 3 5 7 9 10 8 6 4 2
ISBN 0-525-46685-1

For Jamie, who reminded me about hand shadows

The moon rose, fat and white.
Its light fell through James's window,
making a square on the wall.
A breeze blew the curtains—flip-flap—
making shadows.
They rustled—shhhh-shhhh.
To James the shadows looked like . . .

MONSTERS!

"MAMA! DADDY!" yelled James.

"Those were only curtain shadows," said Mama.
James hid his face. "Make them go away," he said.
So Daddy pinned the curtains back,
and the monsters went away.

"Look," said Daddy. "We can make our own shadows."

"We can?" said James.

"Yes," said Mama. "We can make all kinds of animals.
I can make a snail—and look, here's a goose."

Daddy said, "I can make a bird and a dog.
I can even make an alligator."

James laughed. "Can you make an elephant?"

Daddy thought for a minute. Then he made an elephant.

"Mama and I can make a story with these animals."

"It's not a scary story, is it?" asked James.

"Not at all," said Mama.

So Mama and Daddy began to tell a story.

Once upon a time, there were two spiders.
"We can scare anyone," they said.

Snail came along. Slide–slide.
The spiders ran to scare him.

Snail said, "I'm not afraid,"
and popped into his shell.

Bird flew by. Flap–flap.

The spiders ran to scare him.
"You can't scare me. I will fly away," said Bird.

Goose walked by. Honk–honk.

The spiders ran to scare her.
"I will snip–snap both of you," said Goose.
"I'm not afraid of you."

Dog walked by. Bow-wow.

The spiders ran to scare him.
"Ha-ha. Bow-wow. I can run
faster than you," said Dog.

Alligator with his big jaws walked by.
Chop-chop.

The spiders ran to scare him.
"Ha-ha. Chop-chop. You don't scare me."
Alligator snapped his jaws.
The little spiders were scared. "Help, help!"

Elephant was walking by and heard them.
He took them on his trunk and waved them high
in the air.
"Now we are bigger than anyone, even Alligator,"
they said.
Everyone laughed. Ha-ha.

Then Daddy scooped up James and held him high.
"Now I am bigger than anyone," said James.
"Even Daddy," said Mama.
Then Daddy twirled James like an airplane
and flew him into bed.

Mama tucked him in, and they both kissed James
good night and left the room.

The room felt empty.
It was quiet.
It was dark—all but the white square on the wall.
James felt very small without Daddy holding
him high.

He put one finger in the light.

Then he put all his fingers in the light.

Then he put his head and shoulders in the light.

Then James put his whole self in the light.

James jumped and jumped.

And each time, he made a great big . . .

SHADOW

MONSTER!

James was no longer afraid.
He remembered how good he felt after Mama
and Daddy had said good night to him.
Then, all alone in his quiet room, James said,

"Good night, spiders."

"Good night, Bird."

"Good night, Snail."

"Good night, Goose."

"Good night, Dog."

"Good night, Alligator."

"Good night, Elephant."

Then James slipped out of bed and
closed the curtains.
They blew—flip-flap.
James heard them whisper—shhhh-shhhh—
as he crawled into bed.

And James fell asleep.
Fast asleep.
Shhhhhhh.

AFTERWORD

Like James, you too can make shadows. All you need is a dim room, a light source, a smooth pale wall, and hands.

Shadow play is probably the oldest form of theater, starting with pre-historic cave dwellers casting shadows from firelight and moonlight. If you see shadows being cast from moonlight, then the moon is bright enough for you to make your own figures. You make figures by putting your hands between the light source and the wall. If you are using your own light source—a flashlight or a lamp—try putting it from two to five feet from the wall, depending on the strength of the light. The closer you place your hands to the wall, the smaller and sharper your shadows will be. For larger, fuzzier shadows, move your hands away from the wall and closer to the light. Before you begin, warm up your fingers by moving them.

Start by making some of the easier figures, like the dog and the goose. These are made with one hand. Use the figures in this book as models. Try holding one hand, then two, in the light. Wiggle your fingers. Twist your hands for differing angles. Let the shadows lead you into surprise shapes. Often, unintended but wonderful shapes present themselves. Make up your own stories for your shadow figures. Have fun!

THE END